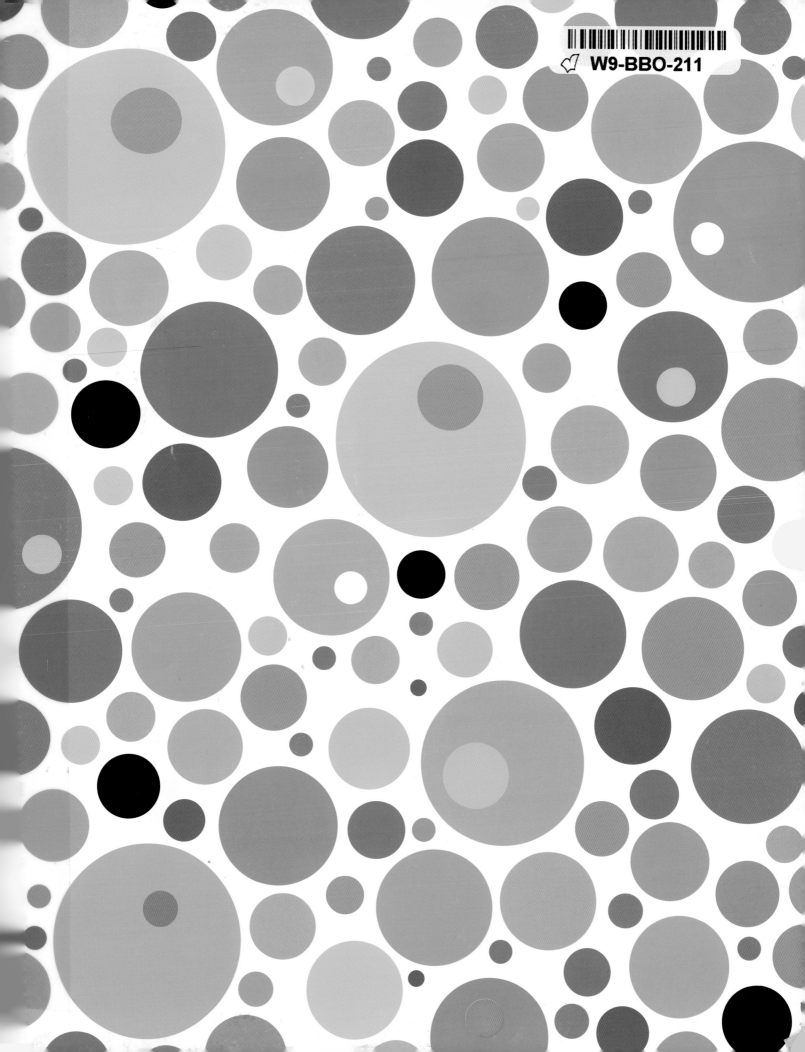

To my kiddos, Daniele and Drew

Library of Congress Cataloging-in-Publication Data available.
ISBN 978-0-8118-7715-2

Book design by Craig Frazier.
Typeset in Serifa Standard 55.
The illustrations in this book were rendered in Adobe Illustrator.

Manufactured by Toppan Leefung, Da Ling Shan Town, Dongguan, China, in June 2010.

10 9 8 7 6 5 4 3 2 1

This product conforms to CPSIA 2008.

Chronicle Books LLC
680 Second Street, San Francisco, California 94107

www.chroniclekids.com

LOTS OF DOTS

Craig Frazier

chronicle books · san francisco

Some dots are big,

some dots are small.

Some dots float,

and some dots fall.

There are dots for going,

and dots for licking,

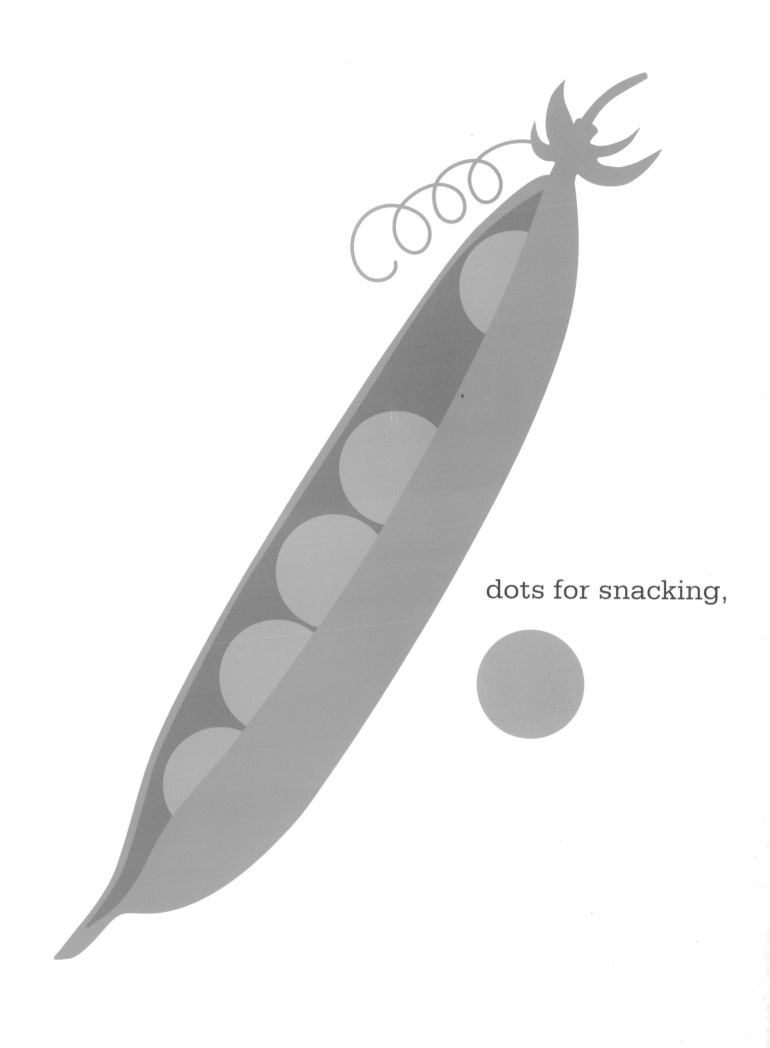

dots for snacking,

and dots for kicking.

Some dots are heavy,

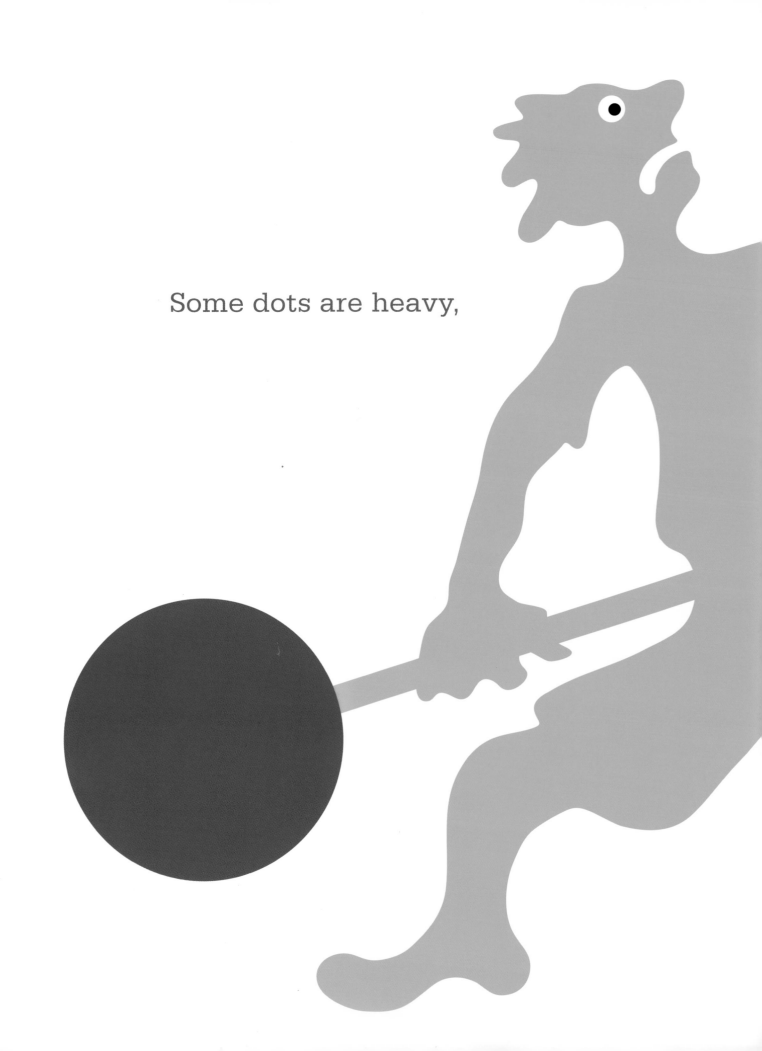

some dots are light,

some dots are colorful,

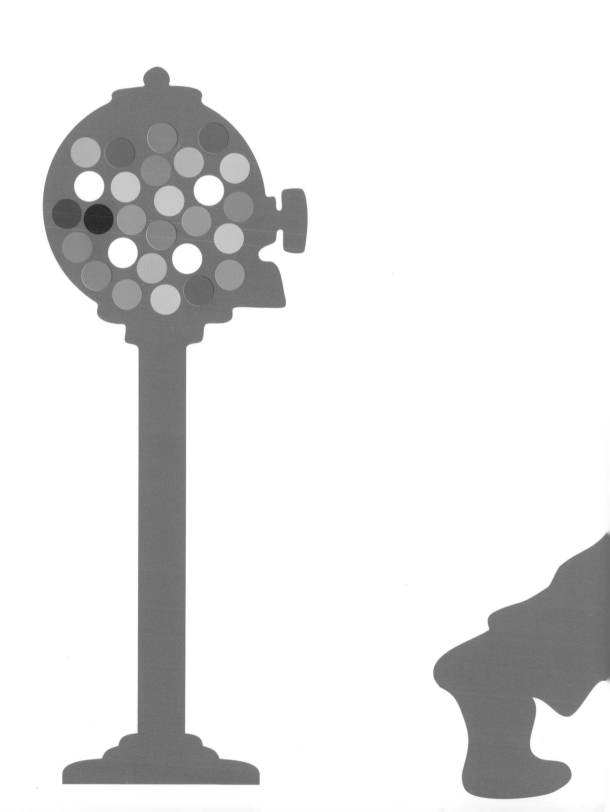

and some dots are bright.

There are dots on shirts,

dots for the sun,

dots that smell sweet,

and dots that are fun.

There are dots on dogs,

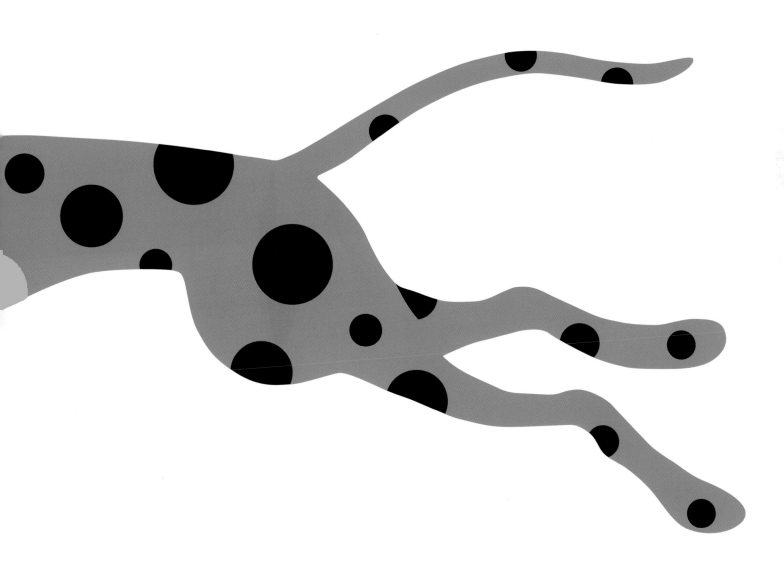

and dots in the air.

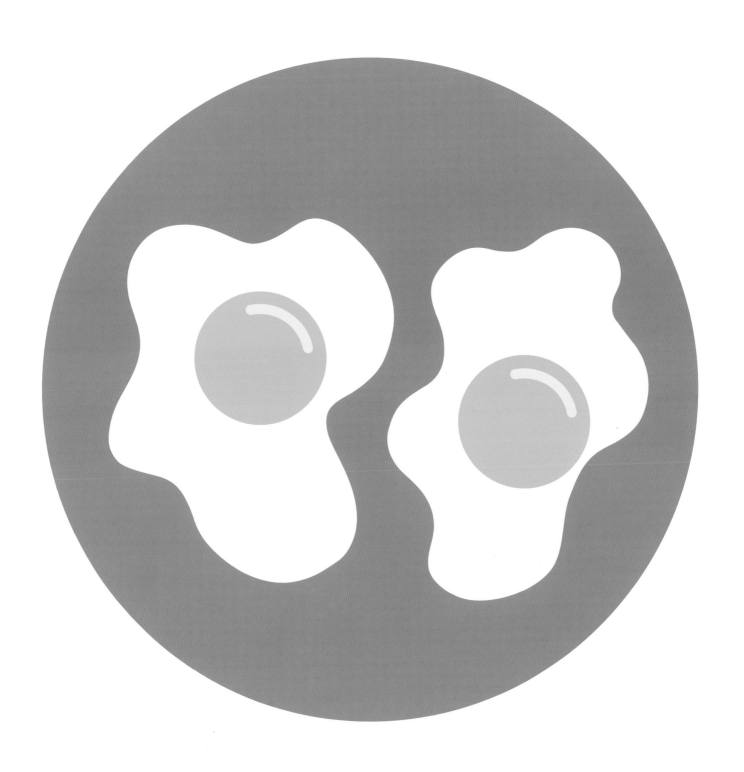

There are dots on your plate.

There are dots everywhere!